Always Alex

Library of Congress Card Number: 98-060544

Illustrations by Kathleen Mullinnix
Book design by Robert Brekke

ISBN: 1-56550-081-4

Published by
Vision Books International
Mill Valley, CA 94941
415.451.7188

Printed in Hong Kong

Always Alex

Written by Heather Fahy Serrano
Illustrated by Kathleen Mullinnix

Vision Books International

Lauren-
make all your
dreams come true!
always
Heather Fahy
Serrano

This story is dedicated to all little girls all over the world, that they may dream, grow, learn and enjoy life.

Thank you to Teresa for prodding me to write;
to Jim for his patient support and for being
really easy to feed at night;
to Matt for his inspiration and encouragement;
to Robin for taking care of all my computer crises;
and to Gregory for being such a delightful
excuse for taking time to play.

And, of course, to Alex. I do this for her, always.

Always, Alex was a joy to be around. She was every mother's dream because of her sunny and friendly nature. But, she never liked to wear pants. Dresses were what she preferred. Dresses were a hint that something special was right around the corner and Alex wanted to be dressed and ready for whatever it was.

Alex was tall for her age. She had a fabulously freckled nose, deep blue eyes and long, straight, brown hair that had a mind of its own. "She's going to be pretty special when she grows up," her mother always thought.

There was a spring in Alex's step and a song on her lips. The house was filled with music whenever she was around.

Alex usually played with three particular dolls. She liked these dolls very much because they agreed with everything she said. She felt they were special because they were so pretty. They had long legs, and perfectly painted lips. She would spend hours dressing them in fancy clothes and tying silk ribbons in their long curly hair.

Alex kept very busy with her dolls, discussing her plans for the future. There was a lot to discuss. After all, when she grew up, she wanted to be a princess just like those in her favorite books and movies.

With her three friends by her side, Alex gathered flowers from her mommy's garden and arranged small bouquets in her tea cups. She placed them here, there and everywhere throughout the house. "Princesses need to surround themselves with pretty things," Alex always thought.

One day as Alex's mother was admiring a small bouquet on the coffee table, she asked her daughter, "Why do you want to grow up to be a princess? Is it to be just like your dolls?"

Alex answered, "My dolls are so pretty and they get to wear beautiful dresses. Besides, a princess always gets to marry a prince!"

Although Alex's mother loved her daughter's imagination and creativity, this bothered her. She was beginning to notice that even at her daughter's young age, she spent too much time worrying about her looks in front of the mirror, fixing her hair and clothes.

She decided to talk to her about this when she put her to bed that night.

That evening her mother read one of her favorite bedtime stories about a beautiful princess who sang all day while she did her chores. In the end, she married a prince and lived happily ever after. Alex's mother realized where her daughter was getting her ideas.

When the story was finished, her mother said, "I know these books are fun to read, but you do understand that it's just make believe, don't you?"

"When you grow up, there will be many things that interest you. You might want to be a teacher, or a doctor. I know you love flowers, so you might want to work in a flower shop. You could become a dancer or travel around the world and write."

"You may change your mind often. Whatever it is you decide to do, you will need to work hard and enjoy your work. You have to make your own dreams come true. That is what will make you happy."

"Real life is different from life in the storybooks. Just because someone does not look like a princess, or one of your dolls, does not mean she is not pretty. The most important thing is not how a person looks, but how a person behaves. I want you to worry about being beautiful on the inside, not the outside. Be kind and thoughtful to others. Always treat people the way you want to be treated."

They were quiet for a moment and then her mother asked, "Do you understand some of what I'm telling you, Alex?" "Yes, mommy," she answered.

Alex's mother decided that she had talked enough for one evening, so she kissed her daughter on the forehead, said, "Sweet dreams," and "Goodnight."

The next morning while Alex was eating breakfast her mother said, "Alex, you have a birthday coming up soon. Let's go shopping today and pick out some invitations and party favors. What kind of party do you want this year?"

She answered quickly and with much delight, "I want a princess party!" Her mother felt a little discouraged, but decided not to bring up last night's talk. Alex was still young and it was probably too much for her to understand.

One of her special companions went to the store with them, and together they picked out princess party invitations, matching crowns, pink candy and balloons with flowers painted on them. She could not wait for her party!

*E*ight of Alex's school friends were invited to celebrate her birthday. All of her guests had on their finest party clothes.

They had a marvelous time eating the princess cake, drinking pink punch and playing games.

They all enjoyed pretending to be princesses wearing their crowns.

After the cake, Alex opened her presents. She was delighted with her new books, puzzles, games and a new pair of rollerblades.

Her mother and father had given her a special, surprise gift. When the party was over, Alex spent the rest of the afternoon outside riding her new turquoise bike.

In the days that followed the party, Alex woke up early each morning. She had so many new things to play with that she couldn't wait to get out of bed.

She invited friends over to play board games. With her mother's help, she practiced rollerblading.

She also enjoyed her quiet time alone putting together the new puzzles. Some were real challenges because they had more pieces than her old ones. She also liked to time herself when she put the smaller ones together.

Another great thing about having a birthday and growing one year older was that Alex could join the local girls' soccer team. She eagerly looked forward to the afternoon practices and Saturday matches.

She was making new friends and inviting them to sleep over at her house. Some of them brought their bikes and they rode together.

At school Alex had a new computer teacher and was learning to play reading and math games on the class computer. She liked to type her name in different sizes and watch it being printed.

When her class had art lessons, Alex learned that she loved to paint pictures of huge fields of flowers and draw big puffy clouds in chalk. Sometimes she got to use the easel and paint with very thick and very thin brushes.

A few weeks after the party, Alex's mother gave her a big empty box. She knew what this box was for because she always got one after each birthday and Christmas.

The box was to take to her bedroom where she was to gather all of the toys she no longer wanted.

Afterward, she and her mother would take the box to the local children's shelter to donate them.

It was never easy for Alex to decide which things to give away, but in the end, she always filled the box.

After Alex finished sorting through her things, she went back outside to ride her bike. Her mother went to her room to get the box so she could put it in the car.

She was surprised at what she saw. The box was filled and at the very top were two of her daughter's favorite dolls. Alex's mother felt terrible. Because of their talk, her daughter must have thought she should give her dolls away.

When she carried the box outside, she called, "Alex, it's wonderful that you are being so generous by giving away your dolls, but I know how special they are to you. If you would like to keep them, I will understand."

Always, Alex thought things through. Slowly she said, "You know mommy, I really thought I wanted to be a princess when I grew up.

"But the ones in my books don't get to ride bikes or rollerblade. They don't get to play sports. They don't go to birthday parties or even go to school. They don't go to the park or have any friends.

"My dolls were really fun to play pretend with, but I don't have much time for that any more. I decided to give those dolls away and let someone else have as much fun as I had dressing and playing with them."

"I kept one to have on my dresser. I still think she's pretty and I like to look at her sometimes."

Alex's mother was very proud of her daughter, but she had to ask, "Well, what happened to the prince you were going to marry?"

"Mom, I can't marry a prince. I don't even like boys!" Alex yelled back to her mother as she rode off to her next adventure.

Like always.